5

j398
J122

Jack the giant killer.
    Jack the giant-killer, [by] Joseph
Jacobs.   Illus. by Fritz Wegner.
N. Y., Walck, c1970.
                                4.95

                I.Jacobs, Joseph.

7-75

JACK THE GIANT-KILLER

Joseph Jacobs

Jack the Giant-Killer

illustrated by
FRITZ WEGNER

HENRY Z. WALCK, INC.
NEW YORK

Text © Kathleen Lines 1970
Illustrations © Fritz Wegner 1970
All rights reserved
ISBN: 0-8098-1185-5
Library of Congress Catalog Card Number: 70-158866
Printed in the United States of America

When good King Arthur reigned, there lived near the Land's End of England, in the county of Cornwall, a farmer who had one only son called Jack. He was brisk and of ready, lively wit, so that nobody or nothing could worst him.

In those days the Mount of Cornwall was kept by a huge giant named Cormoran. He was eighteen feet in height, and about three yards round the waist, of a fierce and grim countenance, the terror of all the neighbouring towns and villages. He lived in a cave in the midst of the Mount, and whenever he wanted food he

5

would wade over to the mainland, where he would furnish himself with whatever came his way. Everybody at his approach ran out of their houses, while he seized on their cattle, making nothing of carrying half a dozen oxen on his back at a time; and as for their sheep and hogs, he would tie them round his waist like a bunch of tallow-dips. He had done this for many years, so that all Cornwall was in despair.

One day Jack happened to be at the town-hall when the magistrates were sitting in council about the giant. He asked: "What reward will be given to the man who kills Cormoran?" "The giant's treasure," they said, "will be the reward." Quoth Jack: "Then let me undertake it."

So he got a horn, shovel, and pickaxe, and went over to the Mount in the beginning of a dark winter's evening, when he fell to work, and before morning had dug a pit twenty-two feet deep, and nearly as broad, covering it over with long sticks and straw. Then he strewed a little mould over it, so that it appeared like plain ground. Jack then placed himself on the opposite side of the pit, farthest from the giant's

lodging, and, just at the break of day, he put the horn to his mouth, and blew, Tantivy, Tantivy. This noise roused the giant, who rushed from his cave, crying: "You incorrigible villain, are you come here to disturb my rest? You shall pay dearly for this. Satisfaction I will have, and this it shall be, I will take you whole and broil you for breakfast." He had no sooner uttered this, than he tumbled into the pit, and made the very foundation of the Mount to shake. "Oh, Giant," quoth Jack, "where are you now? Oh, faith, you are gotten now into Lob's Pound, where I will surely plague you for your threatening words; what do you think now of broiling me for your breakfast? Will no other diet serve you but poor Jack?" Then having tantalised the giant for a while, he gave him a most weighty knock with his pickaxe on the very crown of his head, and killed him on the spot.

Jack then filled up the pit with earth, and went to search the cave, which he found contained much treasure. When the magistrates heard of this they made a declaration he should henceforth be termed

JACK THE GIANT-KILLER,

and presented him with a sword and a belt, on which were written these words embroidered in letters of gold:

"Here's the right valiant Cornish man,
Who slew the giant Cormoran."

The news of Jack's victory soon spread over all the West of England, so that another giant, named Blunderbore, hearing of it, vowed to be revenged on

Jack, if ever he should light on him. This giant was
the lord of an enchanted castle situated in the midst of
a lonesome wood. Now Jack, about four months
afterwards, walking near this wood in his journey to
Wales, being weary, seated himself near a pleasant
fountain and fell fast asleep. While he was sleeping the
giant, coming there for water, discovered him, and
knew him to be the far-famed Jack the Giant-Killer

by the lines written on the belt. Without ado, he took Jack on his shoulders and carried him towards his castle. Now, as they passed through a thicket, the rustling of the boughs awakened Jack, who was strangely surprised to find himself in the clutches of the giant. His terror was only begun, for, on entering

the castle, he saw the ground strewed with human bones, and the giant told him his own would ere long be among them. After this the giant locked poor Jack in an immense chamber, leaving him there while he went to fetch another giant, his brother, living in the same wood, who might share in the meal on Jack.

After waiting some time Jack, on going to the window, beheld afar off the two giants coming towards the castle. "Now," quoth Jack to himself, "my death or my deliverance is at hand." Now, there were strong cords in a corner of the room in which Jack was, and two of these he took, and made a strong noose at the end; and while the giants were unlocking the iron gate of the castle he threw the ropes over each of their heads. Then he drew the other ends across a beam, and pulled with all his might, so that he throttled them. Then, when he saw they were black in the face, he slid down the rope, and drawing his sword, slew them

both. Then, taking the giant's keys, and unlocking the rooms, he found three fair ladies tied by the hair of their heads, almost starved to death. "Sweet ladies," quoth Jack, "I have destroyed this monster and his brutish brother, and obtained your liberties." This said he presented them with the keys, and so proceeded on his journey to Wales.

Jack made the best of his way by travelling as fast as he could, but lost his road, and was benighted, and could find no habitation until, coming into a narrow

valley, he found a large house, and in order to get shelter took courage to knock at the gate. But what was his surprise when there came forth a monstrous giant with two heads; yet he did not appear so fiery as the others were, for he was a Welsh giant, and what he did was by private and secret malice under the false show of friendship. Jack, having told his condition to the giant, was shown into a bedroom, where, in the dead of night, he heard his host in another apartment muttering these words:

"Though here you lodge with me this night,
You shall not see the morning light:
My club shall dash your brains outright!"

"Say'st thou so," quoth Jack; "that is like one of your Welsh tricks, yet I hope to be cunning enough for you." Then, getting out of bed, he laid a billet in the bed in his stead, and hid himself in a corner of the room. At the dead time of the night in came the Welsh giant, who struck several heavy blows on the bed with his club, thinking he had broken every bone in Jack's skin. The next morning Jack, laughing in his sleeve, gave him hearty thanks for his night's lodging. "How have you rested?" quoth the giant; "did you not feel anything in the night?" "No," quoth Jack, "nothing but a rat, which gave me two or three slaps with her tail." With that, greatly wondering, the giant led Jack

to breakfast, bringing him a bowl containing four gallons of hasty pudding. Being loth to let the giant think it too much for him, Jack put a large leather bag under his loose coat, in such a way that he could convey the pudding into it without its being perceived. Then, telling the giant he would show him a trick, taking a knife, Jack ripped open the bag, and out came all the hasty pudding. Whereupon, saying, "Odds

splutters her nails, hur can do that trick hurself," the
monster took the knife, and ripping open his belly,
fell down dead.

Now, it happened in these days that King Arthur's only son asked his father to give him a large sum of money, in order that he might go and seek his fortune in the principality of Wales, where lived a beautiful lady possessed with seven evil spirits. The king did his best to persuade his son from it, but in vain; so at last gave way and the prince set out with two horses, one loaded with money, the other for himself to ride upon. Now, after several days' travel, he came to a market-town in Wales, where he beheld a vast crowd of people gathered together. The prince asked the reason for it, and was told that they had arrested a corpse for several large sums of money which the

deceased owed when he died. The prince replied that it was a pity creditors should be so cruel, and said: "Go bury the dead, and let his creditors come to my lodging, and there their debts shall be paid." They came, in such great numbers that before night he had only twopence left for himself.

Now Jack the Giant-Killer, coming that way, was
so taken with the generosity of the prince that he
desired to be his servant. This being agreed upon, the

next morning they set forward on their journey to-gether, when, as they were riding out of the town, an old woman called after the prince, saying, "He has owed me twopence these seven years; pray pay me as well as the rest." Putting his hand into his pocket, the prince gave the woman all he had left, so that after their day's food, which cost what small store Jack had by him, they were without a penny between them.

When the sun got low, the king's son said: "Jack, since we have no money, where can we lodge this night?"

But Jack replied: "Master, we'll do well enough, for I have an uncle lives within two miles of this place; he is a huge and monstrous giant with three heads; he'll fight five hundred men in armour, and make them to fly before him."

"Alas!" quoth the prince, "what shall we do there? He'll certainly chop us up at a mouthful. Nay, we are scarce enough to fill one of his hollow teeth!"

"It is no matter for that," quoth Jack; "I myself will go before and prepare the way for you; therefore stop here and wait till I return." Jack then rode away at full speed, and coming to the gate of the castle, he knocked so loud that he made the neighbouring hills resound. The giant roared out at this like thunder: "Who's there?"

Jack answered: "None but your poor cousin Jack."

Quoth he: "What news with my poor cousin Jack?"

He replied: "Dear uncle, heavy news, God wot!"

"Prithee," quoth the giant, "what heavy news can come to me? I am a giant with three heads, and besides thou knowest I can fight five hundred men in armour, and make them fly like chaff before the wind."

"Oh, but," quoth Jack, "here's the king's son a-coming with a thousand men in armour to kill you and destroy all that you have!"

"Oh, cousin Jack," said the giant, "this is heavy news indeed! I will immediately run and hide myself, and thou shalt lock, bolt, and bar me in, and keep the keys until the prince is gone." Having secured the giant, Jack fetched his master, when they made themselves heartily merry whilst the poor giant lay trembling in a vault under the ground.

Early in the morning Jack furnished his master with a fresh supply of gold and silver, and then sent him three miles forward on his journey, at which time the prince was pretty well out of the smell of the giant. Jack then returned, and let the giant out of the vault, who asked what he should give him for keeping the

castle from destruction. "Why," quoth Jack, "I want nothing but the old coat and cap, together with the old rusty sword and slippers which are at your bed's head." Quoth the giant: "You know not what you ask; they are the most precious things I have. The coat will keep you invisible, the cap will tell you all you want to know, the sword cuts asunder whatever you strike, and the shoes are of extraordinary swiftness. But you have been very serviceable to me, therefore take them with all my heart." Jack thanked his uncle, and then went off with them. He soon overtook his master and they quickly arrived at the house of the lady the prince sought, who, finding the prince to be a suitor, prepared a splendid banquet for him. After the repast was concluded, she told him she had a task for him. She wiped his mouth with a handkerchief, saying: "You must show me that handkerchief to-morrow morning, or else you will lose your head." With that she put it in her bosom. The prince went to bed in great sorrow, but Jack's cap of knowledge informed him how it was to be obtained. In the middle of the night she called upon her familiar spirit to carry her to Lucifer. But Jack put on his coat of darkness

and his shoes of swiftness, and was there as soon as she was. When she entered the place of the demon, she gave the handkerchief to him, and he laid it upon a shelf, whence Jack took it and brought it to his master, who showed it to the lady next day, and so saved his life. On that day, she gave the prince a kiss and told him he must show her the lips tomorrow morning that she kissed last night, or lose his head.

"Ah!" he replied, "if you kiss none but mine, I will."

"That is neither here nor there," said she; "if you do not, death's your portion!"

At midnight she went as before, and was angry with the demon for letting the handkerchief go. "But now," quoth she, "I will be too hard for the king's son, for I will kiss thee, and he is to show me thy lips." Which she did, and Jack, when she was not standing by, cut off Lucifer's head, brought it under his invisible coat to his master, and the next morning pulled it out by the horns before the lady. This broke the enchantment and the evil spirit left her, and she appeared in all her beauty. They were married the next morning, and soon after went to the Court of King Arthur, where Jack for his many great exploits, was made one of the Knights of the Round Table.

Jack soon went searching for giants again, but he had not ridden far, when he saw a cave, near the entrance of which he beheld a giant sitting upon a block of timber, with a knotted iron club by his side. His goggle eyes were like flames of fire, his countenance grim and ugly, and his cheeks like a couple of large flitches of bacon, while the bristles of his beard resembled rods of iron wire, and the locks that hung down upon his brawny shoulders were like curled snakes or hissing adders. Jack alighted from his horse, and, putting on the coat of darkness, went up close to the giant, and said softly: "Oh! are you there? It will not be long before I take you fast by the beard." The giant all this while could not see him, on account

of his invisible coat, so that Jack, coming up close to the monster, struck a blow with his sword at his head, but, missing his aim, he cut off the nose instead. At this, the giant roared like claps of thunder, and began to lay about him with his iron club like one stark mad. But Jack, running behind, drove his sword up to the hilt in the giant's back, so that he fell down dead. This done, Jack cut off the giant's head, and sent it, with his brother's also, to King Arthur, by a waggoner he hired for that purpose.

Jack now resolved to enter the giant's cave in search of his treasure, and, passing along through a great many windings and turnings, he came at length to a large room paved with freestone, at the upper end of which was a boiling caldron, and on the right hand a large table, at which the giant used to dine. Then he came to a window, barred with iron, through which he looked and beheld a vast number of miserable captives, who, seeing him, cried out: "Alas! young man, art thou come to be one amongst us in this miserable den?"

"Ay," quoth Jack, "but pray tell me what is the

meaning of your captivity?"

"We are kept here," said one, "till such time as the giants have a wish to feast, and then the fattest among us is slaughtered! And many are the times they have dined upon murdered men!"

"Say you so," quoth Jack, and straightway un-locked the gate and let them free, who all rejoiced like condemned men at sight of a pardon. Then searching the giant's coffers, he shared the gold and silver equally amongst them and took them to a neighbouring castle, where they all feasted and made merry over their deliverance.

But in the midst of all this mirth a messenger brought

news that one Thunderdell, a giant with two heads, having heard of the death of his kinsmen, had come from the northern dales to be revenged on Jack, and was within a mile of the castle, the country people flying before him like chaff. But Jack was not a bit daunted, and said: "Let him come! I have a tool to

pick his teeth; and you, ladies and gentlemen, walk out into the garden, and you shall witness this giant Thunderdell's death and destruction."

The castle was situated in the midst of a small island surrounded by a moat thirty feet deep and twenty feet wide, over which lay a drawbridge. So Jack employed men to cut through this bridge on both sides, nearly to the middle; and then, dressing himself in his invisible coat, he marched against the giant with his sword of sharpness. Although the giant could not see Jack, he smelt his approach, and cried out in these words:

> "Fee, fi, fo, fum!
> I smell the blood of an Englishman!
> Be he alive or be he dead,
> I'll grind his bones to make me bread!"

"Say'st thou so," said Jack; "then thou art a monstrous miller indeed."

The giant cried out again: "Art thou that villain who killed my kinsmen? Then I will tear thee with my teeth, suck thy blood, and grind thy bones to powder."

"You'll have to catch me first," quoth Jack, and
throwing off his invisible coat, so that the giant might
see him, and putting on his shoes of swiftness, he ran
from the giant, who followed like a walking castle, so

that the very foundations of the earth seemed to shake at every step. Jack led him a long dance, in order that the gentlemen and ladies might see; and at last to end the matter, ran lightly over the drawbridge, the giant, in full speed, pursuing him with his club. Then, coming to the middle of the bridge, the giant's great weight broke it down, and he tumbled headlong into the water, where he rolled and wallowed like a whale. Jack, standing by the moat, laughed at him all the while; but though the giant foamed to hear him scoff, and plunged from place to place in the moat, yet he could not get out to be revenged. Jack at length got a cart rope and cast it over the two heads of the giant and drew him ashore by a team of horses, and then cut off both his heads with his sword of sharpness, and sent them to King Arthur.

After some time spent in mirth and pastime, Jack, taking leave of the knights and ladies, set out for new adventures. Through many woods he passed, and came at length to the foot of a high mountain. Here, late at night, he found a lonesome house, and knocked at the door, which was opened by an aged man with a head as white as snow. "Father," said Jack, "can you lodge a benighted traveller that has lost his way?"

"Yes," said the old man; "you are right welcome to my poor cottage." Whereupon Jack entered, and down they sat together, and the old man began to speak as follows: "Son, I see by your belt you are the great conqueror of giants, and behold, my son, on the top of this mountain is an enchanted castle; this is kept by a giant named Galligantua, and he, by the help of an old conjurer, betrays many knights and ladies into his castle, where by magic art they are transformed into sundry shapes and forms. But above all, I grieve for a duke's daughter, whom they fetched from her father's garden, carrying her through the air in a burning chariot drawn by fiery dragons, when they secured her within the castle, and transformed her into a white hind. And though many knights have tried to break the enchantment, and work her deliverance, yet no one could accomplish it, on account of two dreadful griffins which are placed at the castle gate and which destroy everyone who comes near. But you, my son, may pass by them undiscovered, where on the gates of the castle you will find engraven in large letters how the spell may be broken." Jack gave the

old man his hand, and promised that in the morning
he would venture his life to free the lady.

In the morning Jack arose and put on his invisible
coat and magic cap and shoes, and prepared himself
for the fray. Now, when he had reached the top of
the mountain he soon discovered the two fiery
griffins, but passed them without fear, because of his

invisible coat. When he had got beyond them, he found upon the gates of the castle a golden trumpet hung by a silver chain, under which these lines were engraved:

> "Whoever shall this trumpet blow,
> Shall soon the giant overthrow,
> And break the black enchantment straight;
> So all shall be in happy state."

Jack had no sooner read this but he blew the trumpet, at which the castle trembled to its vast foundations, and the giant and conjurer were in horrid confusion, biting their thumbs and tearing their hair, knowing

their wicked reign was at an end. Then the giant stooping to take up his club, Jack at one blow cut off his head; whereupon the conjurer, mounting up into the air, was carried away in a whirlwind. Then the enchantment was broken, and all the lords and ladies who had so long been transformed into birds and beasts returned to their proper shapes, and the castle vanished away in a cloud of smoke. This being done, the head of Galligantua was likewise, in the usual manner, conveyed to the Court of King Arthur, where, the very next day, Jack followed, with the knights and ladies who had been delivered. Whereupon, as a reward for his good services, the king prevailed upon the duke to bestow his daughter in marriage on honest Jack. So married they were, and the whole kingdom was filled with joy at the wedding. Furthermore, the king bestowed on Jack a noble castle, with a very beautiful estate thereto belonging, where he and his lady lived in great joy and happiness all the rest of their days.

The earliest known date for this story is 1711, when J. White of Newcastle-on-Tyne, issued his chapbook, 'Jack and the Giants'. Other chapbooks then read by children were romantic legends—like 'Bevis of Southampton' and 'Guy of Warwick'—so it would seem that 'Jack the Giant-Killer' was the first of English folk tales to be printed.

Jacobs' sources were two nineteenth-century chapbooks, with 'some hints from Felix Summerly's version'. It is evidence of his artistry and integrity that in his retelling he keeps the humour, vigour and forthright expressions of earlier versions.

Lang (in *The Blue Fairy Book*, 1889) used 'an old chapbook', and said that a good version was 'hard to procure'. This inferior retelling can hardly have been from the sources used by Jacobs.

Someone who read 'Jack' as a child was a certain Robert Bloomfield. In maturity he recalled only 'its abominable absurdities'. This opinion was shared by Mrs Trimmer (and also, much later, by Samuel Goodrich—the American 'Peter Parley'—who denounced Halliwell's collections and specifically attacked 'Jack the Giant-Killer'). These two, with others of a similar puritan taste, were so successful in their efforts to exclude everything 'miraculous and fabulous' from books for children, that by the time Newbery published his first children's book in 1744, 'Jack' and his kind had been banished, and it was his successor, Harris, who gradually re-introduced them. Early in the nineteenth century the didactic writers, greatly influenced by 'Peter Parley', again succeeded in dislodging fairy tales. But Felix Summerly (Sir Henry Cole) publicly criticised Goodrich, and deliberately set out to 'cultivate the affections, fancy and imagination of children' in his *Home Library*. The first twelve little booklets, all with reputable texts, were published between 1841 and 1849, and the first title of all was 'Jack the Giant-Killer'.

Some copies of chapbooks survived long past their time, and Felix Summerly's discriminating choice of stories became the nucleus of future collections, still constantly reprinted, so 'Jack', proving indestructible, has had a continuous life in print for nearly three hundred years.

Although the first fairy tales to be published individually were from *The Arabian Nights* and from Perrault, their companion 'Jack the Giant-Killer' has never been other than completely British. In every version, good or bad, Jack is a Cornishman; he travels through Wales; sends his grisly trophies to King Arthur, and is rewarded by the king. In some accounts he becomes one of the Knights of the Round Table, but nowhere is he ever known as 'Sir' Jack. True to his humble origin, he remains simply—Jack.

Fritz Wegner's illustrations not only convey the native folk element but also suggest, without caricature, the humour inherent in the story. The giants *are* ferocious and cruel, but they are also stupid. Cocky Jack is never afraid. It is as much by cunning stratagem as by prowess that he outwits and overcomes them. Here is a picture-story of giants for tough little boys that should not alarm little girls. KATHLEEN LINES